Makeshift Miracle

BOOK 1: THE GIRL FROM NOWHERE

Story:
JIM ZUB

Art:
SHUN HONG CHAN

This book is dedicated to my brother Joe,
who introduced me to anime and manga
way back when.
~Jim

Being able to work on Makeshift Miracle is an important event in my life. It has somewhat changed the way I will conceive art in the future. I would like to dedicate this book to all the friends and family that have always given me their support!
~Hong

Makeshift Miracle

BOOK 1: THE GIRL FROM NOWHERE

CHAPTER 1:
Impact

CHAPTER 2:
Long Walk Home

CHAPTER 3:
Home Invasion

CHAPTER 4:
Daydreams & Phone Calls

CHAPTER 5:
Roots & Other Attachments

CHAPTER 6:
Falling Down, Fading Through

Chapter One:
Impact

My name's Colby Reynolds...
and if life is a journey, I got lost
somewhere along the way.

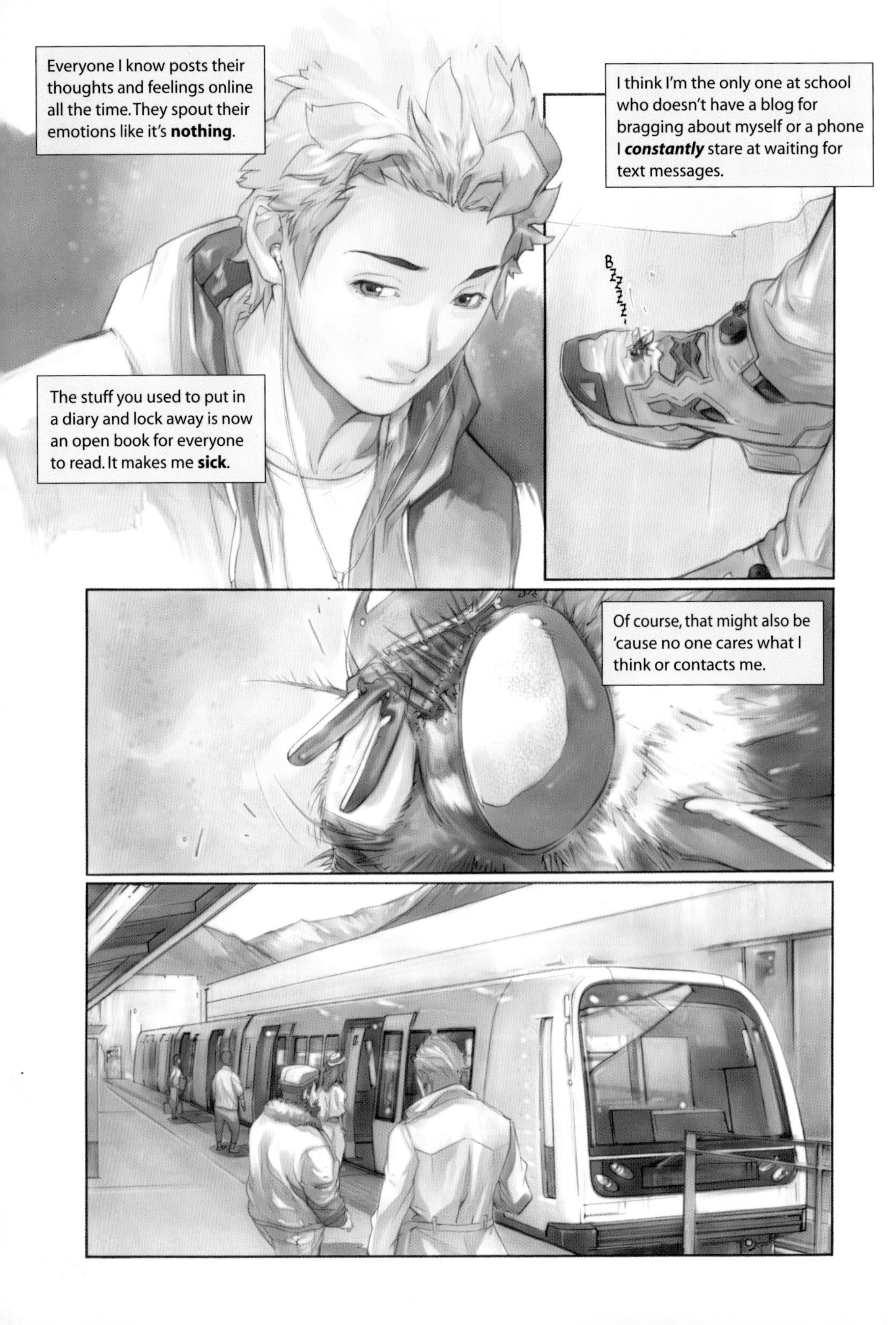
Everyone I know posts their thoughts and feelings online all the time. They spout their emotions like it's **nothing**.
I think I'm the only one at school who doesn't have a blog for bragging about myself or a phone I ***constantly*** stare at waiting for text messages.
The stuff you used to put in a diary and lock away is now an open book for everyone to read. It makes me **sick**.
BZZZZZ-
Of course, that might also be 'cause no one cares what I think or contacts me.

I'm just typing all this as fast as I can to try and make sense of it. I'm not going to post it anywhere so I guess it doesn't even matter but maybe it'll help organize my thoughts.
Tonight's been just... ***unbelievable***. I don't know what else to call it.
SHOVE
HEY!
People suck.
No one cares if you're smart or nice. The world wants everyone to be average and selfish.
The vacation you deserve!
This week I get to be selfish too. I can go where I want and do what I want.

My parents went away on vacation. Somewhere tropical, I don't remember. Does it even matter?
The point is that they're not here. For the first real time in my life, I'm on my own.
I know other people at school would throw a house party or break in to the liquor cabinet.
It sounds dumb, but all I wanted to do after school was wander around without a curfew and explore the city by myself.
At the time I thought I was trying to clear my head. Now, I know differently...
I was being ***lured*** to something out of control.

It was like being in a dream. I didn't choose the direction...
Esurio is the Answer
...or plan the route.
Eye Safety is Vision for the Future
SO WHAT'RE YOU TRYING TO SAY?
I DON'T CARE, OKAY?! LEAVE IF YOU WANNA LEAVE.
YOU DID NOT! YOU DON'T HAVE THE GUTS.

I just followed it.
--GET HOME, EH?
DOES IT REALLY MATTER?
HEH, PROBABLY NOT.

Until I found just
the right spot...

It was so calm and beautiful.
I watched as the sun went down
and the city lights slowly turned on.

...and then something glimmered in the sky.
SHOOTING STAR?
It moved so fast...

...and when that thing
struck from the sky,
everything changed.

UUHHHH...
OH, MAN.

I couldn't believe
I wasn't dead.
THAT WAS, JUST... WOW.

Every logical thought I had told me I should *run*.
It could be dangerous. I could be hurt.
SSSSSSSSSS~
But I didn't go. I walked *towards* it, perfectly calm.

Everything changed.

Chapter Two:
Long Walk Home

A girl fell from the sky
like a comet.

NO WAY...
DID... ANYONE ELSE... SEE...
JUST... WOW...

UH... C... OLD...

COLD? OH GEEZ, OF COURSE!
I was so shocked that I didn't even think about the weather. My heart was pounding. I couldn't feel the cold at all.
I didn't want to move her in case something was broken but I couldn't let her freeze.
IT'S GONNA BE OKAY. I'LL FIND HELP AND YOU'LL BE OKAY.
UH...
What could I do? Everything was a blur.

IS ANYONE OUT THERE?! I NEED HELP!
THERE'S SOMEONE HURT!
ANYONE?

Everyone always wonders how they'll react in an emergency... If they'll have their head together enough to be effective.
I couldn't find my backpack with my cell phone inside.
I had no way to call for help. I could barely think.
NO NO NO...
What would you do?
I knew we had to go. Maybe a paramedic wouldn't have done it that way, in case she broke bones or something, but I couldn't leave her there lying in the snow.
OKAY, HERE GOES NOTHING.
I was surprised at how light she felt.
I was running on adrenaline and couldn't feel pain or the weight of her in my arms at all.

She was strangely beautiful at that moment and... sort of familiar. It felt like we knew each other.
Was she someone from my school?
I... I'M GONNA GET YOU SOMEWHERE SAFE.

IS THIS EVEN REALLY *HAPPENING?*
I'M CARRYING A GIRL WHO FELL FROM THE SKY.
SAYING THAT OUT LOUD MAKES IT SOUND *INSANE.*

OF COURSE, TALKING TO MYSELF OUT LOUD DOESN'T SAY A LOT ABOUT MY MENTAL STATE EITHER...

THIS ISN'T GOOD. I DON'T EVEN KNOW WHICH WAY I'M GOING AND IT'S GETTING COLDER.
JUST NEED TO GET MY BEARINGS... AND THINK *WARM* THOUGHTS.
WARM, WARM, *WARM*...
BAKED POTATO RIGHT OUT OF THE OVEN, STEAK AND GRAVY, HOT APPLE CRUMBLE...
GREAT. THAT DIDN'T WORK. NOW I'M COLD *AND* HUNGRY...

In the back of my mind I knew we could die out in the snow... but it was just like falling asleep.
THIS SUCKS.
I JUST WISH I WAS HOME.

O-OKAY.
WH- WHAT THE-?!

AAAH!

A sudden flash and we were sitting in my kitchen at home.
OKAY, THAT WAS MESSED UP.

Chapter Three: Home Invasion

That girl glowed with a strange light and then, in a flash, we found ourselves sitting in my kitchen at home.
OKAY, THAT WAS MESSED UP.

UUUH?
WHA-? WHERE AM I?
WHERE?
MY HOUSE. WE'RE IN MY HOUSE.
YOU TELEPORTED BOTH OF US HERE IN TO MY KITCHEN.
I DID WHAT?

I, I, I- I DON'T KNOW! I DON'T KNOW HOW YOU DID THAT OR WHY, BUT YOU DID!
I MEAN... AR- ARE YOU RADIOACTIVE OR SOMETHING?
ARE YOU AN ALIEN?!
OKAY, OKAY... LET'S JUST CALM DOWN HERE.
I DON'T KNOW HOW THIS HAPPENED. I'M CONFUSED TOO. DON'T WIG OUT.
UH... WHY AM I NAKED?
THAT IS NOT WHAT IT LOOKS LIKE! I FOUND YOU THAT WAY! YOU WERE OUT COLD IN THE MIDDLE OF THE PARK... IN THE SNOW! LYING IN THE SNOW IN A CRATER, NAKED AND ASLEEP OR SOMETHING!
DID YOU SAY "IN A CRATE"? I WAS IN A BOX?
NO, NOT A "CRATE", A "CRATER". Y'KNOW... BIG HOLE IN THE GROUND. YOU FELL OUT OF THE SKY LIKE A METEOR AND CRASHED IN TO THE GROUND. CRATER.
I KNOW IT SOUNDS TOTALLY INSANE, BUT YOU DID.

A NAKED METEOR?
YEAH!
LOOK, IF YOU'RE RADIOACTIVE MAYBE YOU SHOULD JUST STAY IN THERE AND DO STUFF UNTIL YOU FEEL BETTER... OR WHATEVER.
I AM NOT RADIOACTIVE! STOP FREAKING OUT... WHOEVER YOU ARE.
I... I'M COLBY.
MY NAME'S COLBY.
AND YOU ARE...?
IRIS.

OKAY, IRIS. COOL.
LOOK, I DON'T KNOW EXACTLY HOW IT HA--
I FEEL CRAPPY, DIRTY AND COLD. I'M GONNA TAKE A SHOWER, IF THAT'S OKAY WITH YOU.
UH... YEAH. SURE. I GUESS.
TOWELS AND CLOTHES UPSTAIRS?
YUP.
There was a naked meteor girl in my house.
Of course she needed a shower. Silly me.

I thought for a sec
she might be joking.
She wasn't.
She casually went
upstairs and grabbed a
shower, just like that.
FWOOOSSSSSHHHHHH
Who was this girl?
How did she survive that crash...
and teleport us both here?
FWOOOSSSSSHHHHHH

A horrible thought suddenly entered my mind. What if she was some kind of experiment, or a mutant criminal?
Am I in ***danger?***
Should I call the police?

What could I say?
Would they even ***believe*** me?
I couldn't do it.
I had to talk to her and find out how this all happened.

ALL DONE.
WERE YOU CALLING FOR A PIZZA?
THAT WAS QUICK.
I THOUGHT ABOUT ORDERING FOOD, BUT I DON'T KNOW WHAT YOU LIKE... AND I DON'T HAVE A CREDIT CARD ANYWAYS.
OH! UH... I THOUGHT YOU WERE GONNA GRAB CLOTHES?
I WILL WHILE YOU'RE GETTING CLEANED UP. AND THEN I'LL GET SOME DINNER GOING. GOT ANY SOUP?
PROBABLY... BUT YOU DON'T KNOW WHERE ANYTHING IS IN THE KITCHEN.
I'M SURE I CAN FIGURE OUT YOUR KITCHEN.
GO FORTH AND CLEANSE THE DIRT.
GO, GO!
I couldn't believe she was bossing me around in my own house. I saved her life!
OKAY.

None of it felt real. It was like I was sleepwalking through the entire event, or watching it happen to someone else.
I could feel the little cuts on my face sting.
My body was tired and sore from the hike, but the whole crash and appearing home... it didn't make any sense.
Why am I still ***calm?*** How can I know this whole thing should scare me, but not feel it?
Am I going crazy?

THAT SMELLS REALLY GOOD!
STIR STIR
A PINCH OF OREGANO ADDS A LOT OF DEPTH TO PLAIN OL' TOMATO SOUP.
THIS WILL WARM US BOTH UP AND BATTLE THE BEASTS OF HUNGER GROWLING IN OUR BELLIES.
DEFINITELY.

HEY.
YEAH?
THIS WHOLE THING IS NUTS. I NEED TO KNOW HOW YOU GOT HERE... WHAT THIS IS ALL ABOUT. I- I DON'T EVEN KNOW WHAT TO SAY.
TELL YOU? I'D TELL YOU IF I **COULD**. THERE'S **NOTHING** TO TELL, COLBY.
ME EITHER! IT'S ALL PRETTY MESSED UP. I DON'T KNOW WHAT TO SAY EITHER.
YOU MEAN YOU'RE NOT GONNA TELL ME?
WHILE YOU WERE GETTING CLEANED UP I THOUGHT ABOUT MAKING UP A CRAZY STORY, SOMETHING TO TRY AND CONNECT THE DOTS, BUT I COULDN'T.
I **DON'T KNOW** HOW ANY OF THIS HAPPENED. EVERYTHING IN MY MIND BEFORE I WOKE UP HERE IS A TOTAL **BLANK**. WELL, BLANK EXCEPT MY NAME... AND, APPARENTLY, MAKING SOUP TASTE BETTER.
THIS IS LIKE A BAD SCI-FI MOVIE.
HEH, YEAH.
IT'S A BAD MOVIE, BUT GOOD SOUP.

SO, IF YOU DON'T REMEMBER ANYTHING THEN YOU'VE OBVIOUSLY GOT NOWHERE TO STAY.
YUP. NO MONEY, NO HOME.
YOU'RE FREE TO CRASH HERE TONIGHT. I'VE GOT SCHOOL TOMORROW, SO I'LL BE GONE ALL DAY, BUT AFTER I GET BACK WE CAN FIGURE OUT HOW WE EXPLAIN ALL THIS TO THE POLICE OR WHATEVER.
THAT'S TOTALLY FAIR. I APPRECIATE IT.
NO PROBLEM. I'LL HEAD UPSTAIRS AND GET MY STUFF READY FOR TOMORROW. YOU CHILL HERE AND GET SOME REST. WE'VE BOTH HAD A WEIRD NIGHT.
OKAY.
That's how Iris, the meteor girl, came to my house.

That's how Iris, the meteor girl, came to my house.
She's asleep on the couch downstairs and I'm wide awake typi
this journal/diary/whatever.
I've got to get up early for school but there's no way I can rest.
There are so many questions and way too much to think about.
How long is she gonna be here? What do I tell Mom and Dad when
they get back from their vacation?
One minute I'm irritated about life and the next I'm dodging aster-
oids or something.
I guess that'll teach me for being in a bad mood.
Maybe I should write this up as a story for my creative wr-
CREATIVE WRITING CLASS... SCHOOL STUFF... AW, CRAP!
I'M SO STUPID! I FORGOT MY BACKPACK IN THE WOODS!

Dream Places
by
Colby Reynolds
The first time I encountered the
in my mind, I didn't
what to make of it. Visions,
creatures... all of them
out to me beyond the
our waking minds keep.
Dreams.

Chapter Four:
Daydreams & Phone Calls

I think everybody feels lost at one point or another. Lost and scared...

We're all looking for confirmation that we're doing the right thing, making the right choices.

Wandering around desperately trying to find the path that will lead us to happiness and fulfillment.

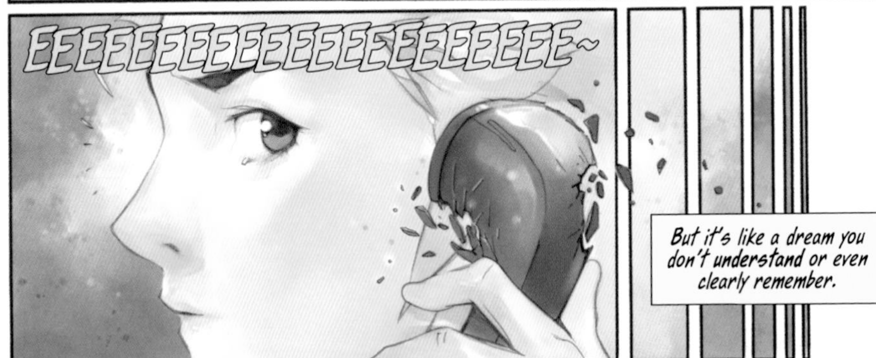
EEEEEEEEEEEEEEEEEEEEEEEE~
But it's like a dream you don't understand or even clearly remember.

~EEEEEEEEEEEE

WHAT WAS THAT?
Little snippets sit in your subconscious, but there's no clarity.

I don't want to wake Iris up. She must really need the sleep.
It feels a bit weird leaving her here and going to school, but I don't know what else to do.
I guess I could skip school, but my parents will be ticked off enough that I wandered around alone and almost died last night. No point in creating even more trouble.
She can rest and we'll figure this out when I get back.

I want to jump up and down screaming, tell everybody I see--
"I was struck by a falling star last night! There's a mystery girl at my house and she fell from the sky!"
HEH.
It sounds stupid, even though it's true.
No one has any idea what I experienced. For them it's just another day.
-AND IF HE DOESN'T TEXT ME BACK, I'M GONNA DIE!
DON'T WORRY, GIRLFRIEND. I'LL SAVE YOU. HA HA HA!

This amazing event happened to me and I can't even tell anyone about it. No one would believe me!

EH? PHONES?

WHAT A WEIRD DREAM...

OH, WHAT'S THIS?

Iris,
I hope you slept well, all things considered.
Feel free to cook some breakfast or whatever.
Make yourself at home as much as possible.
I'll ack after school and then we can
stuff.
Thanks,
Colby
P.S.- If possible, don't do anymore weird
flashy power stuff.

HEY, COLBY. HOW'S IT GOIN'?
HI, BLAKE. I'M... I'M GOOD.
Blake's a nice guy, but but he's always a bit awkward.
DID YOU GET MY TEXTS LAST NIGHT? WHY DIDN'T YOU DROP ME A LINE?
UH... I ACTUALLY LOST MY PHONE. SORT OF WEIRD. HARD TO EXPLAIN.
OH YEAH? WEIRD HOW? IS THERE A GIRL INVOLVED?
YEAH... BUT NOT HOW YOU THINK.
A SECRET GIRL? DO TELL, BUDDY! GIMME ALL THE DETAILS.
UH... YOU WOULDN'T REALLY BELIEVE ME IF I TOLD YOU.

Sitting in class now, I can't even concentrate. I'm still kind of tired and sore. All my homework was in my backpack, so I feel detached from every lecture.
I feel like everything around me is happening on T.V. and I'm watching it instead of participating.

I can feel myself drifting off, but it's not like regular sleep at all.
All of a sudden, I remember...
Everything from my dream is sharp again. I can see it with absolute clarity.
UH...

A phone? Is this some kind of trick?
BZZT BZZT BZZT BZZT

BZZT BZZT BZZT BZZT
INCOMING CALL FROM
VERIDICUS

UH... HELLO?
HELLO? WHO'S THIS NOW?

WHO AM I? YOU CALLED ME!
COLBY REYNOLDS!
HANG UP YOUR CEL PHONE THIS INSTANT OR I'LL KICK YOU OUT OF CLASS!
I NEED YOU TO TELL ME WHO YOU ARE AND HOW YOU CONTACTED ME...
AW, GEEZ.

COLBY, WHERE ARE YOU GOING? IS IT SOME KIND OF EMERGENCY?
UH... YEAH. IMPORTANT CALL. SORRY.
YES, IT IS IMPORTANT. WHO ARE YOU TALKING TO? I NEED YOU TO PAY ATTENTION!
YOU FOUND THE GIRL, RIGHT? THAT'S WHY YOU'RE CALLING.
YOU MEAN IRIS? YEAH, BUT I DIDN'T--
YOU HAVE MADE CONTACT WITH SOMETHING FAR BEYOND YOUR CAPACITY TO UNDERSTAND.
OKAY...
NO, IT'S NOT OKAY! NOT AT ALL! THERE ARE OTHERS SEARCHING FOR HER. SHE WASN'T SUPPOSED TO CROSS BACK OVER. YOU HAVE TO STAY HIDDEN AND CONTROL YOUR DREAMS!
WAIT, I--
CLICK
BZZZZZZZZ

That guy. He said people are looking for Iris.
YO!
EARTH TO COLBY, COME IN COLBY! WHAT'S GOIN' ON, MAN?
HEY! I THOUGHT YOU SAID YOU LOST YOUR CEL PHONE LAST NIGHT!
I'VE GOTTA GO!
WHOMP

What was I thinking?
She came from the sky! Why did I just leave her at the house? I'm so stupid!

YOU'RE GONNA GET YOURSELF KILLED, KID!
Why is all this happening?

Is Iris in danger?
HA, FOUND ALL THE INGREDIENTS FOR DINNER! COLBY'S KITCHEN IS JUST LIKE MINE BACK HOME.
THAT'S WEIRD. I REMEMBER MY KITCHEN?
MAYBE IT IS SOME KIND OF TEMPORARY AMNESIA...
OH, THE PHONE'S RINGING!
ER, MAYBE NOT. I THOUGHT I HEARD IT THOUGH... SUPER WEIRD.

I'LL JUST PREP SOME VEGGIES AND WATCH T.V. UNTIL--
COLB-- AH!
NO WAY...

Chapter Five:
Roots & Other Attachments

The strange voice on my phone told me people are looking for Iris.

I knew this whole thing was weird, that last night was weird. Why'd I pretend any of this was normal? Why'd I go to school and leave her at home alone?
And... why... didn't I practice more in gym class? This run is brutal!

Okay... almost there. Slow down, Colby. Slow down... think, think, think.
No bad sounds. The door's still closed. No broken windows...
Wait! What about Iris?
Last night she glowed with energy and we blinked right across the city! Is she radioactive or something?
Is it even safe for me to go in the house?
This is crazy... Just go in you idiot!

FASCINATING! SO MANY SKYSCRAPERS...
I WONDER IF THEY'VE FINALLY COLONIZED THE MOON.
CRAZY COSPLAY! WHAT A WEIRDO...
YOU THERE! HOW MANY MOON COLONIES ARE THERE? WHAT'S THE LATEST NEWS IN SPACE EXPLORATION?
HUH? SPACE-WHAT?

ASTRONAUTS, MY FRIEND.
YOU DRESSED UP FOR SOME KINDA SCI-FI CONVENTION OR SOMETHIN'?
DOES... THIS 'CONVENTION' YOU'RE TALKING ABOUT INVOLVE OUTER SPACE, EXPLORATION OF SOLAR SYSTEMS AND THE WORLDS BEYOND?
YEAH, TOTALLY!
THEN, YES. I AM HERE FOR THAT. ALL OF IT. TO EXPLORE THIS PLACE AND RETRIEVE ELEMENTS THAT HAVE TRAVERSED HERE UNLAWFULLY.
COOL. HAVE FUN!
HMMM... THAT WASN'T VERY INFORMATIVE.

MAYBE NOW THAT I M *CENTRAL* TO THE POPULATION BASE THE SCANNER WILL PICK UP A *TRAIL*...

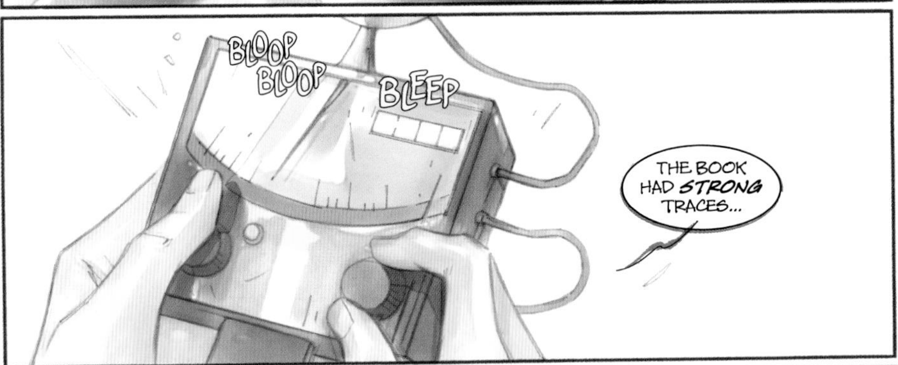
BLOOP
BLOOP
BLEEP
THE BOOK HAD *STRONG* TRACES...

EXCELLENT! LEAD ME TO IT!
ARAGE

A- A-
A- A... A...
TREE!
YOU'RE
HOME!
NEAT, EH?
I MADE MYSELF SOME
BRUNCH AND WHEN I CAME
BACK IN HERE... WELL,
THERE IT WAS!
A TREE?
I'M SURE THERE'S A REASONABLE
EXPLANATION. LET'S HAVE DINNER
AND THEN WE'LL FIGURE OUT
WHAT TO DO WITH IT.
I HOPE YOU
LIKE PASTA WITH
MUSHROOMS!

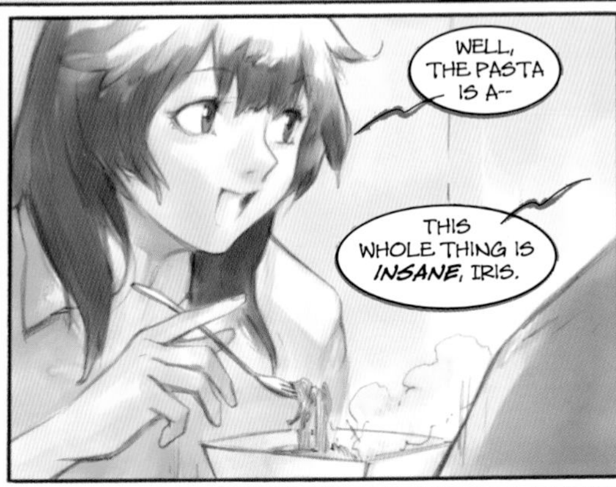
WELL, THE PASTA IS A--
THIS WHOLE THING IS INSANE, IRIS.

THERE'S A TREE GROWING IN THE LIVING ROOM! HOW CAN YOU POSSIBLY ACT LIKE THAT'S NORMAL?!

WHAT WAS I GONNA DO, CHOP IT DOWN BEFORE YOU GOT HOME? RE-CARPET?!
YEAH, THERE'S A TREE. I'M SORRY.

SORRY?! SORRY DOESN'T GET RID OF IT! SORRY DOESN'T EXPLAIN IT! WHERE DID IT COME FROM?!
I DON'T KNOW! HOW WOULD I?! I'M JUST AS IN THE DARK AS YOU ARE, COLBY!
ALL THIS IS FREAKING ME OUT! WHERE DID YOU COME FROM? WHY ARE PEOPLE LOOKING FOR YOU? HOW DID THIS HAPPEN?!
I DON'T KNOW! I DON'T KNOW! I REALLY DON'T!
YOU THINK I'M NOT SCARED?! YOU THINK THIS IS EASY? I WANT ANSWERS! I CAN'T REMEMBER ANYTHING!

I was wrong. I thought Iris was okay because she knew what was going on.
It was just her way of coping. Staying calm because if she didn't, she'd break down.
I'M SCARED TOO...

BLEEP
BLEEP
BLEEP

RUMBLE
OH, LOOKS LIKE SUSPENDED WATER PARTICLES ARE GOING *CUMULONIMBUS*. SOMEBODY'S **NOT** HAPPY...

BLEEP
BLEEP
BLEEP

Iris needed a moment alone. She's really upset. I can't really blame her for that. We're both on edge.
I think it's actually grown over dinner. Crazy.
If this was a horror movie, there'd be dead stuff and blood, or ghosts... something evil. I can't tell if this tree is good, bad or... anything.
It's just here, growing.
I wonder why it has this hole?

CREEEEEEEAK
OH, WOW.
Girls crash from the sky... Phones ring with warnings from strangers... Trees open up doorways to nowhere...
Sure, why not?
IRIS... YOU'VE GOTTA SEE THIS...

I'm sick of waiting to see what other weird things come next.

If nothing makes sense then I'll just embrace the strange... dive in.

Tree hole? Fine.

I'm gonna climb down and see what this is all about.

Even if it's not the best choice, at least I'm making it.

Chapter Six: Falling Down, Fading Through

IRIS... YOU'VE GOTTA SEE THIS...

OKAY, LET ME JUST...
JU... JU... UUUUH...
COLBY...?

Right from the start it was obvious this wasn't a normal tree, but even still... I can't believe this.
How far down does it go?
I should head back up and make sure Iris is okay.
COLBY... COME... BACK...
HUH?
That sounded close! Who s--
CRACK
NO!

Got to--
Can't--
SHHHHHHRIIIC
SNAP
SHHHHHHH

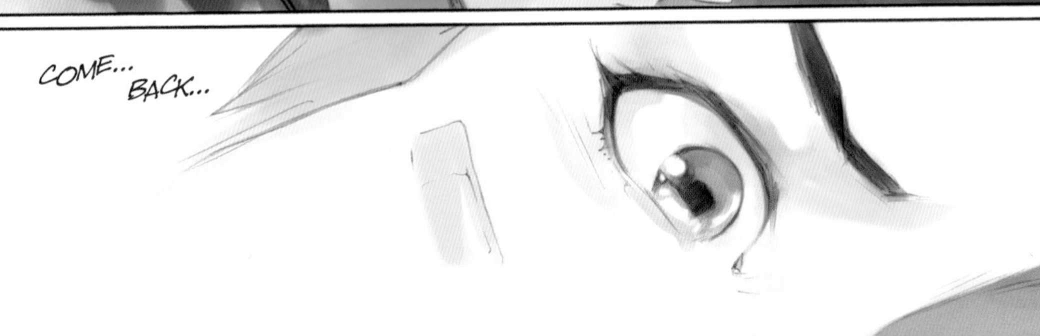
COME... BACK...

I... I...
I CAN'T SEE IT.
WHAT AM I--
NO...
ESCAPE...

When you fall in a dream, you jolt awake, disoriented and confused.
I'm not waking up.
This is no dream.

HOW... HOW LONG HAVE I BEEN HERE?
DID I FIND IT? AM I HOME?
WHY DOES THIS FEEL SO FAMILIAR...
LIKE BREATHING IN MEMORIES...
I THINK I WANTED THIS... TO FADE AWAY... TO BE FORGOTTEN...
IT WAS ME.
I... WISHED FOR IT... AND THEY GRANTED IT.

EXCELLENT!
BLIP-BLIP-BLIP-BLIP
YOU WON'T ESCAPE ME... EVEN HERE IN THIS CRUDE DOMICILE YOU'RE USING FOR SHELTER.
IT'S BEST TO ASSUME SOME HOSTILITIES WILL BE REQUIRED...

NO ONE MOVE! THIS--
BAM

NO, STOP!
STOP, PLEASE...

BLEEEEEEEET

HRRM...
EVERYWHERE I GO ON THIS PLANETOID THERE'S A CURIOUS MIXTURE OF ORGANIC MATERIAL AND CRUDE INERT BUILDING PROPERTIES.
BACKWARDS SCIENTIFIC CONSTRUCTION MEETS COLDLY FUNCTIONAL BLANDNESS. IT'S *SAD*, REALLY.
I WONDER IF THIS DOMICILE CONTAINS EDIBLE OR LIQUID SUSTENANCE.
EVEN BETTER IF IT'S SOMETHING EVEN REMOTELY ***FLAVOURFUL...***

UUUUUH...
I remember falling... then, nothing...
Did I break anything?
OWWW...
Nope. Just really sore.
Not sure exactly how I landed without breaking my neck there.
Light... and a way out?
I hope Iris is okay... I shouldn't have left her there. I don't even know what I was thinking.
I needed answers.

Why's it so quiet? I don't hear anything at all. Not a sound...
OH, WOW.
There's a stillness here, a serenity...

...and, strangely, I don't feel lost at all.

To be continued

Coming in
Makeshift Miracle
BOOK 2: THE BOY WHO STOLE EVERYTHING
In a land of dreams and nightmares, forgotten memories and the secret that binds Iris and Colby together will be revealed.

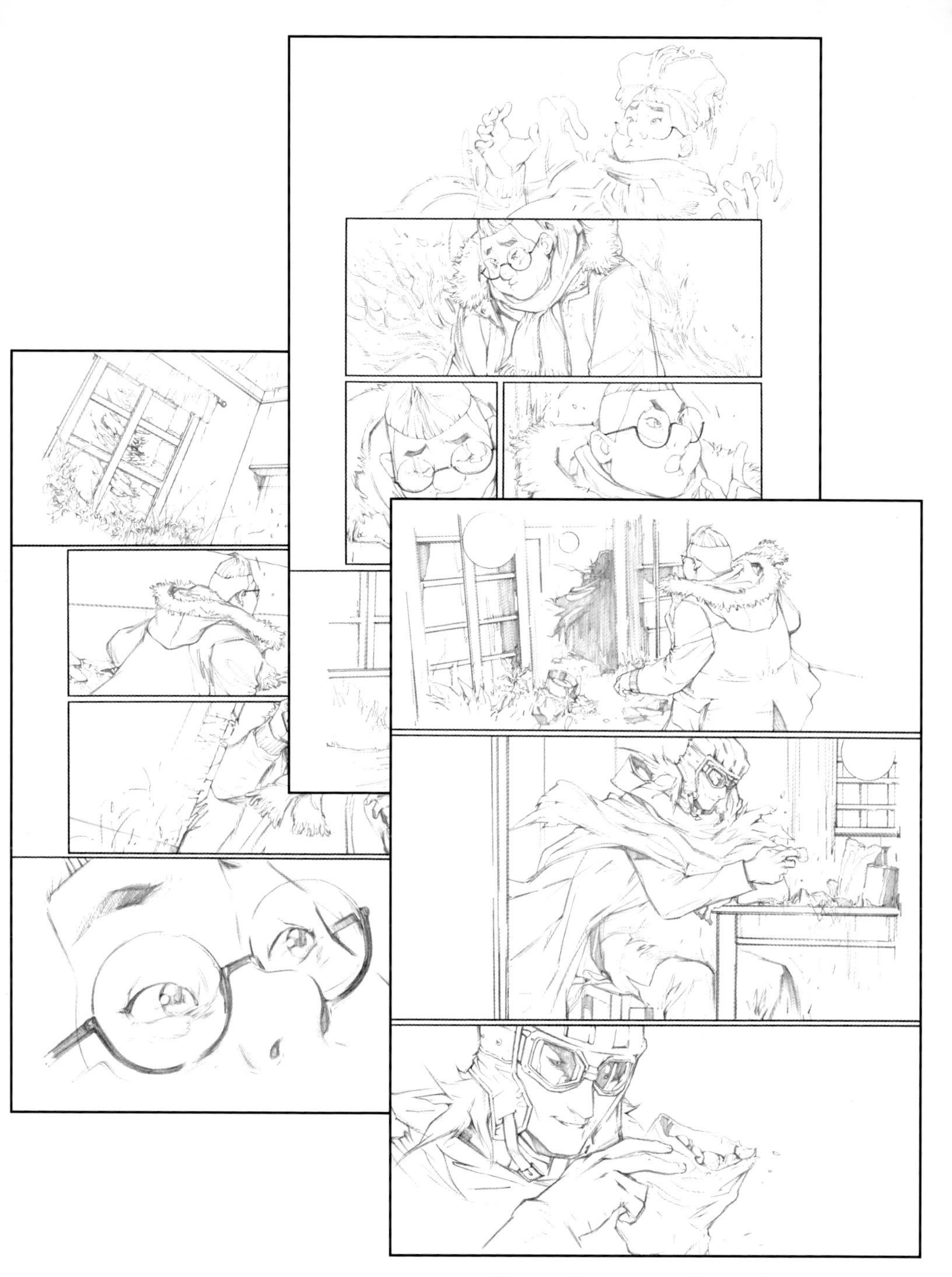

Follow the miracle online at:

MAKESHIFTMIRACLE.COM

SHUN HONG CHAN
SKETCHBOOK

Colby Reynolds

Colby Reynolds

Iris
IRIS.

Blake Matthews

Esurio

STREET FIGHTER LEGENDS
VOL. 3: IBUKI
ISBN-13: 978-1926778136

STREET FIGHTER LEGENDS:
THE ULTIMATE EDITION
ISBN-13: 978-1926778228

SKULLKICKERS VOL. 1:
1000 OPAS AND A DEAD BODY
ISBN-13: 978-1607063667
March 2011 / Image Comics / $9.99 US

SKULLKICKERS VOL. 2:
FIVE FUNERALS AND A BUCKET OF BLOOD
ISBN-13: 978-1607064428
Nov 2011 / Image Comics / $16.99 US

SKULLKICKERS TREASURE TROVE
ISBN-13: 978-1607063742
April 2012 / Image Comics / $34.99

RANDOMVEUS
AN ORIGINAL GRAPHIC NOVEL ADVENTURE!
THIS ISN'T OUR FAULT! WE JUST DELIVER PACKAGES!
GOOD. THAT MONEY AND CHOWDER ARE AS GOOD AS MINE.
FEAR NOT PEOPLE! THE MIGHTY OAK IS HERE!
I'M THE GREATEST BEAN THAT EVER LIVED!

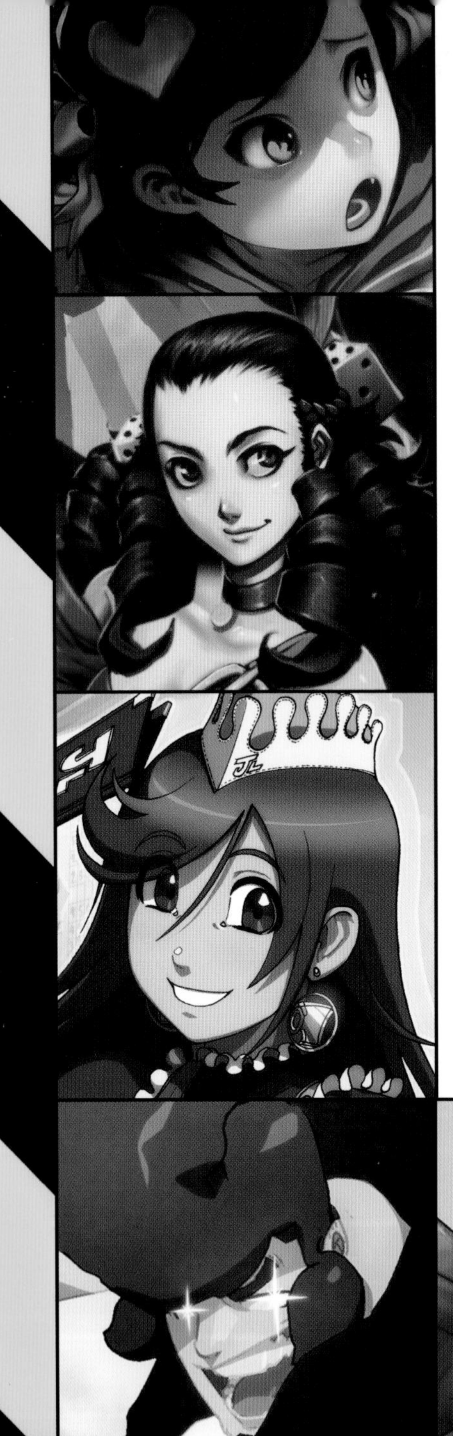

VENT

The artists of UDON let their own creative visions loose in an original anthology artbook - VENT!

VENT features original stories, dozens of never-before-seen illustrations, and extensive tutorials revealing the secrets behind both the traditional and digital creative techniques of the UDON crew.

Featuring:

ALVIN LEE
ANDREW HOU
ARNOLD TSANG
ATTILA ADORJANY
CHRISTINE CHOI
CRYSTAL REID
DAX GORDINE
ERIC KIM
ERIC VEDDER
EMILY WARREN
JAY AXER
JEFFREY CRUZ
JIM ZUB
JOE NG
JOE VRIENS
GENZOMAN
GREG BOYCHUCK
LEO LINGAS
LONG VO
MATT MOYLAN
OMAR DOGAN
RYAN ODAGAWA
SAEJIN OH
STEVEN CUMMINGS

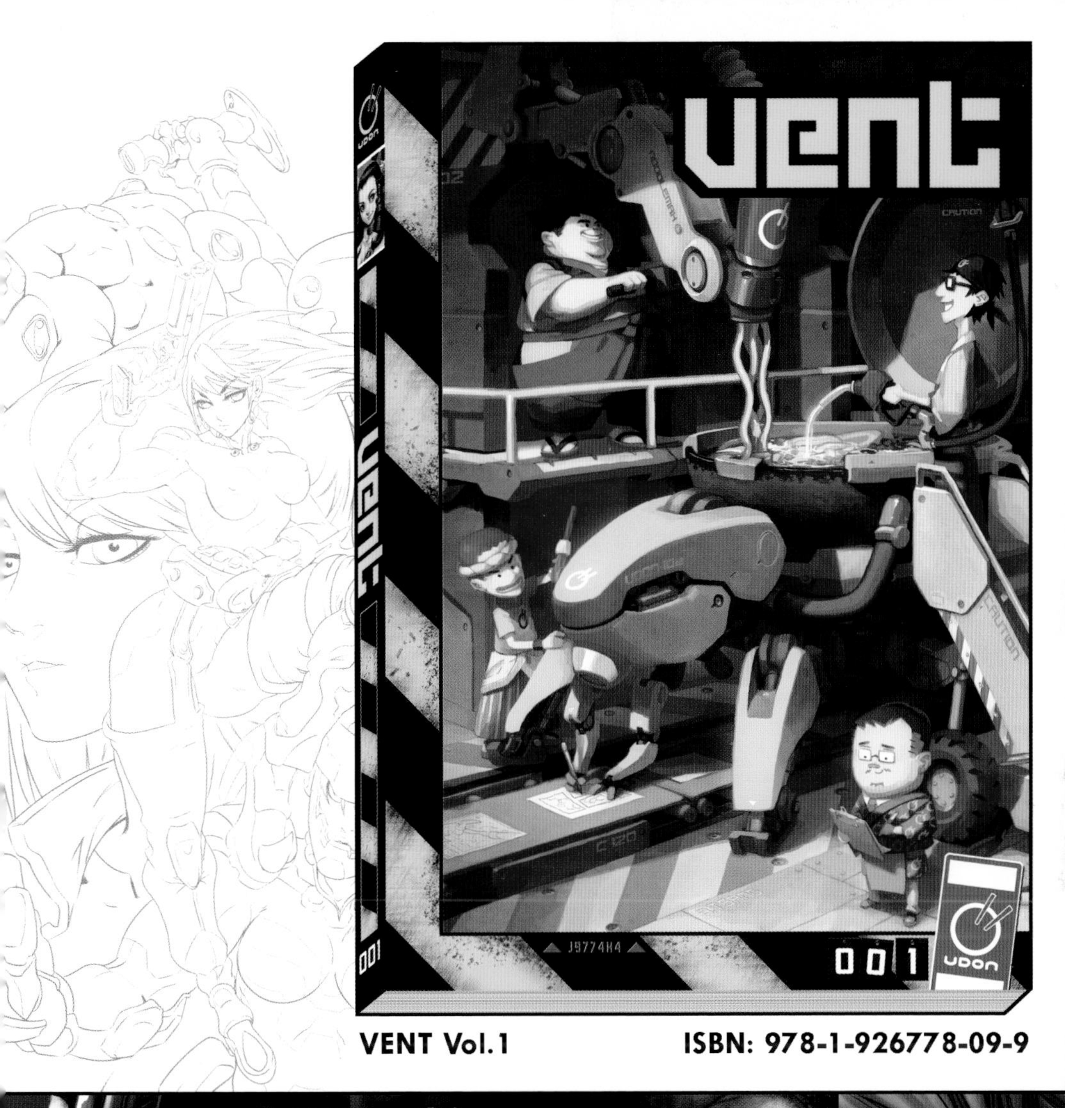
VENT
CAUTION
VENT
001
UDON

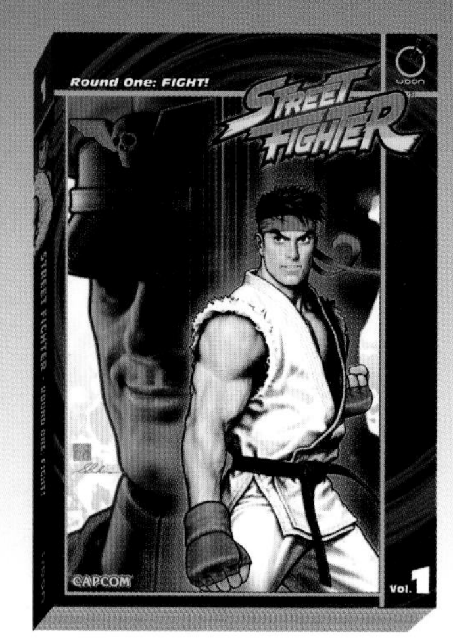

STREET FIGHTER VOL.1 TP
ISBN: 978-1-897376-18-8

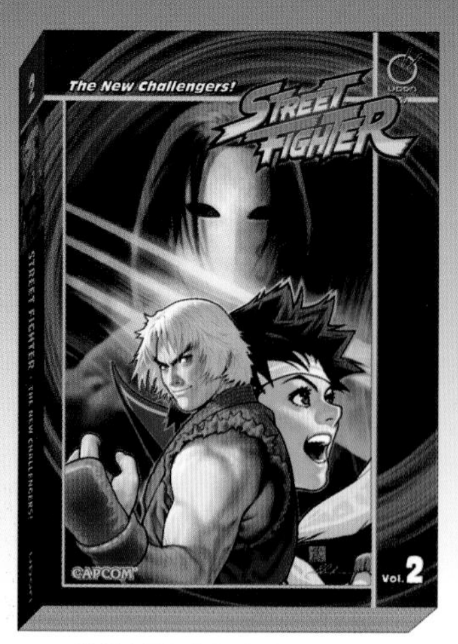

STREET FIGHTER VOL.2 TP
ISBN: 978-0-973865-27-1

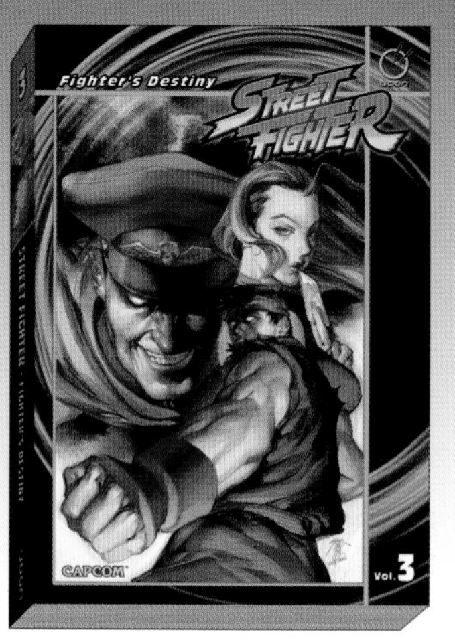

STREET FIGHTER VOL.3 TP
ISBN: 978-0-973865-28-8

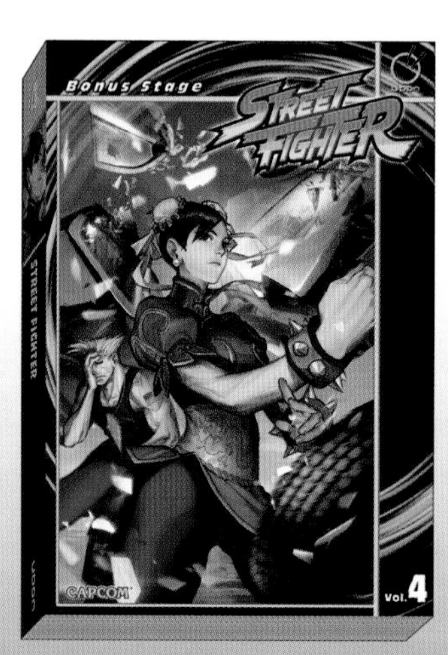

STREET FIGHTER VOL.4 TP
ISBN: 978-1-897376-00-3

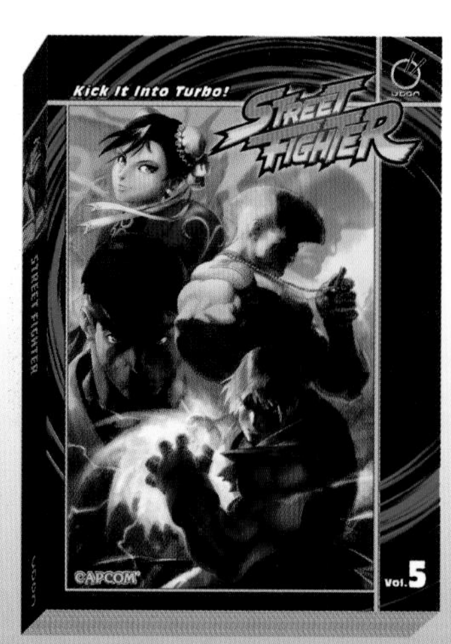

STREET FIGHTER VOL.5 TP
ISBN: 978-1-897376-48-5

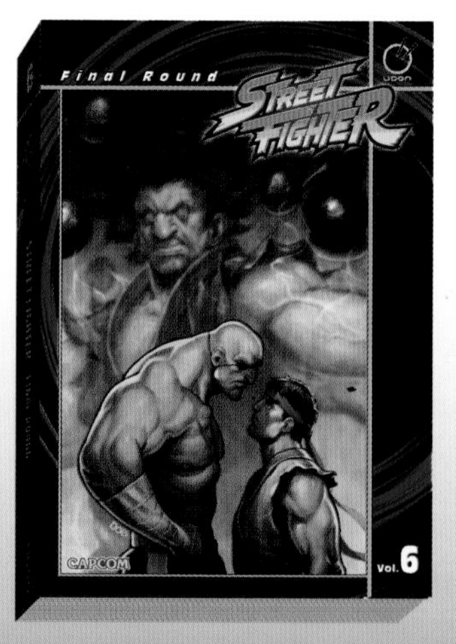

STREET FIGHTER VOL.6 TP
ISBN: 978-1-897376-49-2

COMPLETE YOUR UDON LIBRARY!

STREET FIGHTER LEGENDS:
SAKURA VOL.1 TP
ISBN: 978-0-978138-64-6

STREET FIGHTER LEGENDS:
SAKURA VOL.2 TP
ISBN: 978-0-978138-65-3

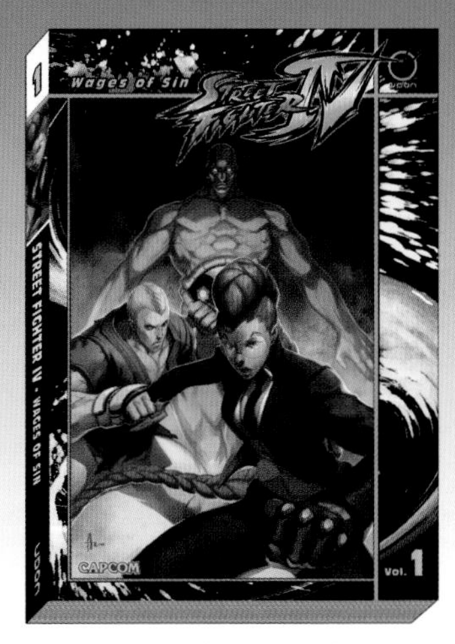

STREET FIGHTER IV VOL.1
ISBN: 978-1-897376-59-1

DARKSTALKERS VOL.1
ISBN: 978-0-973865-21-9

DARKSTALKERS VOL.2
ISBN: 978-1-926778-02-0

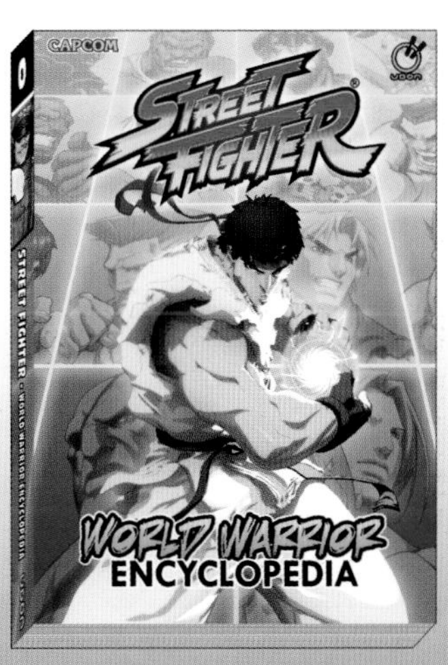

STREET FIGHTER:
WORLD WARRIOR ENCYCLOPEDIA
ISBN: 978-1-926778-01-3

CAPCOM UDON

VOLUME 2

ISBN: 978-1-926778-27-3

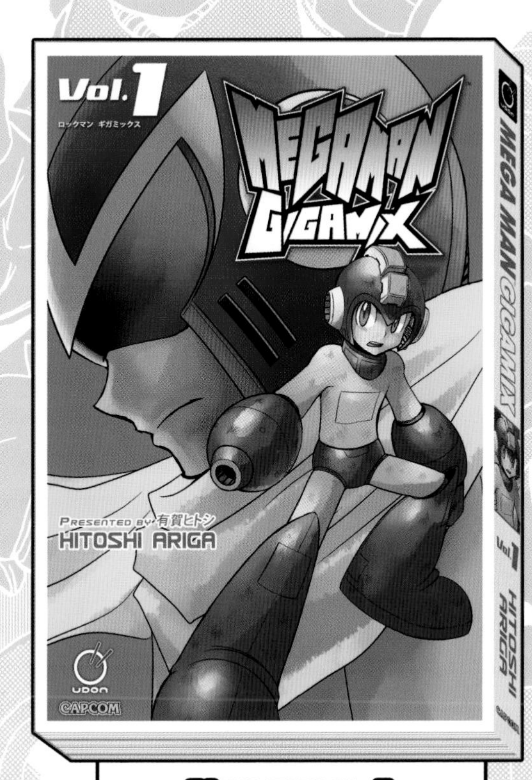

VOLUME 1

ISBN: 978-1-926778-23-5

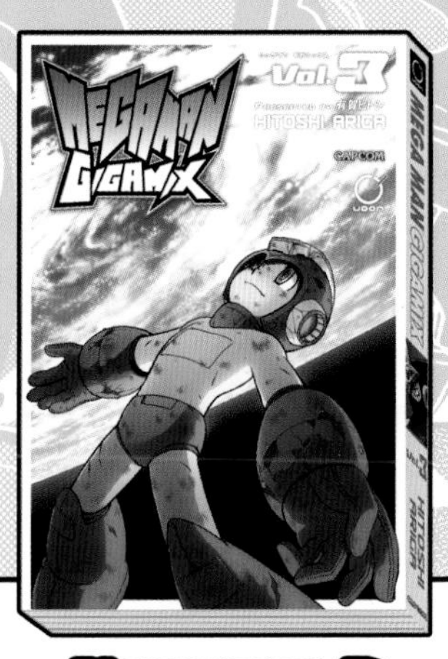

VOLUME 3

ISBN: 978-1-926778-31-0

MEGA MAN™ -GIGAMIX-

Makeshift Miracle

BOOK 1: THE GIRL FROM NOWHERE

Story: JIM ZUB
Art: SHUN HONG CHAN
Letters: MARSHALL DILLON
Script Translation: JULIE LU

UDON STAFF
Chief of Operations ERIK KO
Managing Editor MATT MOYLAN
Project Manager JIM ZUBKAVICH
Director of Marketing CHRISTOPHER BUTCHER
Marketing Manager STACY KING
Associate Editor ASH PAULSEN
Japanese Liaison STEVEN CUMMINGS
Editor, Japanese Publications M. KIRIE HAYASHI

Published by UDON Entertainment Corp.
118 Tower Hill Road, C1, PO Box 20008, Richmond Hill,
Ontario, L4K 0K0, Canada

www.UDONentertainment.com

Printed by Suncolor Printing Co. Ltd. E-mail: suncolor@netvigator.com

First Printing: May 2012
ISBN-13: 978-1-926778-47-1
ISBN-10 : 1-926778-47-2

Printed in Hong Kong